The Garden of Life

A Story of Hope
For All Ages

by

JOHN R. AURELIO

The Garden of Life

A Story of Hope For All Ages

by

JOHN R. AURELIO

illustrated by
MARYAM GOSSLING

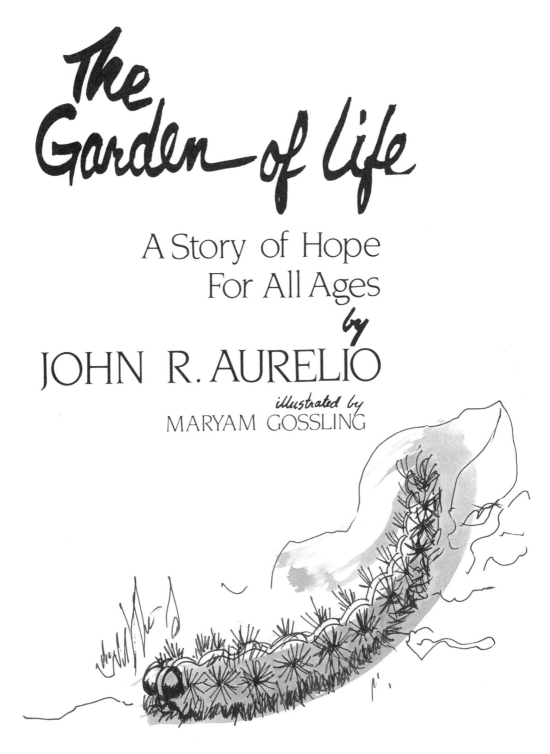

CROSSROAD/NEW YORK

1989

The Crossroad Publishing Company
370 Lexington Avenue
New York, N.Y. 10017

Printed in the United States of America

Library of Congress Cataloging-in-Publication Data

Aurelio, John.
      The garden of life / by John R. Aurelio: illustrated by Maryam
Gossling.
         p.   cm.
      Summary: Dejected because he has no friends, Charlie the
Caterpillar crawls into a dark cave and is transformed by a wondrous
experience.
      ISBN 0-8245-0921-8 (pbk.)
      [1. Fables.   2. Caterpillars—Fiction.   3. Christian life-
Fiction.]   I. Gossling, Maryam, ill.   II. Title.
PZ8.2.A85Gar   1988
      [Fic]—dc19
                                                      88-28284
                                                         CIP
                                                          AC

To Augie,
who is now a
butterfly.

Once upon a time there was a caterpillar. His name was Charlie.

He was Charlie the Caterpillar.

He lived in a
beautiful garden
where there were
colorful
flowers, tall trees
and lots of animals.

Life in the garden was wonderful.
Charlie loved the sun because it
made him warm and comfortable,
and it made his fur coat
shiny and prettier.

He loved the sweet
smell of the
flowers in the
afternoon breeze.

8

But most of all, Charlie loved all the
wonderful animals that lived
in the garden.

There were fuzzy, furry
rabbits that played among
the flowers.

There were tall and graceful deer that grazed in the grass. There were dogs that chased one another around the trees and cats that climbed the trees whenever the dogs came running. All in all it was a wonderful place to be and it was great to be alive.

Everything in the garden was perfect, except for one thing. Charlie was all alone.

There were no other caterpillars like him and he didn't have a friend.

One fine day Charlie decided that he didn't want to be alone any longer. He would go out and find a friend.

Charlie knew exactly where to go to look for a friend. Slowly, he inched his way over to the pond where all the animals came for a drink.

When he finally got there he
didn't have to wait long before some
rabbits came hopping by.

"Hi!" Charlie called out to them.
The rabbits stopped when they
heard him call. They bent over
and wriggled their noses
at him.

"What do you want?"
one of them asked.

"Can I be your
friend?" Charlie asked.

"You? Our
friend?" they
laughed.

"You want to be
our friend?" They rolled
in the grass giggling and
pointing at poor little
Charlie.

"Sure. Why not?"
said one of the rabbits.
"Just hop along with
us," he snickered.
Then all the rabbits
began hopping
round and round,

laughing and shouting,
"Come hop with us.
Come hop with us."

"I can't," Charlie said hanging
his head sadly. "I can't hop."

17

"Well then," one of them said. "You better grow some feet if you want to keep up with us. Big feet."

"Yes. Big feet! Big feet!" they laughed and hopped away leaving Charlie all
alone.

Charlie felt crushed for the first time in his life. The rabbits had not been kind. But, he wasn't going to let that discourage him. He still had hope that he would find a friend. Someone else was bound to come along. Someone kinder than the rabbits.

It wasn't long before a young deer came down to the pond to drink. The deer seemed very tall to Charlie, but that was no reason for them not to be friends. He would ask her.

"Hello!" he shouted at the top
of his lungs to make sure the deer
could hear him.

The young deer
lifted her head quickly.
Her body tensed while
her nose sniffed the air.

Charlie shouted out again
even louder. "Hello! I'm down here."
The deer looked down and saw Charlie
in the grass. She relaxed a little bit.
"Hello," she
answered.

"I was just wondering,"
Charlie smiled to show
that he was friendly. The
deer still looked rather
tense. "I'm all alone and
I would like very much
to have a friend.
Would you be my
friend?

"I would be happy to be your friend,"
the deer said, "but, you have no legs. You
would have to have very strong legs to
keep up with me. We might have to
run at a moment's notice if there's
any danger."

"There's nothing to worry about here,"
Charlie said.

"Maybe for you," the deer said lifting
her head and sniffing the air again.

At just that moment a twig snapped
and before Charlie could say another word
the deer bolted away as fast as lightning.

Charlie couldn't see what had frightened the deer away but when he saw how fast she ran, he knew that the deer was right.

Without legs he could never be her friend. Once again he was sad.

"I must find a friend," he said to himself. "Life is no fun without a friend." Just then, a magpie landed on a bush near by.

The bird began to sing a beautiful, sweet song. Charlie listened to the music until his heart felt happy again.

"I will ask the bird to be my friend," he said.

Charlie crawled over to the bush and called out. "Would you like to be my friend?"

The bird cocked her head and looked at Charlie sideways. "What was that you said?"

"I said I want to be your friend."

"You? You? You want
to be my friend? Why you're a
caterpillar. You can't be my friend," the bird
replied. "No sir! No siree! It can't be done. First
of all, you can't sing, now, can you?"

It was true. Charlie couldn't sing. He never thought about it before.

"Well, I don't suppose that's so terribly, awfully important," the bird rattled on. "There are some birds I know that can't sing. And there are some I know that can sing and shouldn't sing. What's more important is that you don't have wings. If you don't have wings you can't fly. Although, I do hear tell that there are some birds who do have wings but can't fly. Now, that's a fine state of affairs. To have wings and not be able to fly. I would have nothing to do with them, let me tell you. And you! You haven't got a wing to your name. Obviously, you can't fly, can you?"

Charlie was all confused by the bird's rambling on and on. But, one thing he was certain of — he didn't have wings and he couldn't fly.

"No, I can't fly."

"Can't fly. Can't fly. That's the trouble with most of the animals around here. They can't fly. They can run and they can hop. they can swim and crawl and leap. But, they can't fly. What good is all that if you can't fly? Well, of course, I may not be able to do all those things myself, but, it doesn't really matter if you can fly. And I can fly and you can't. So there you have it."

Charlie couldn't keep up with the magpie's conversation let alone with the magpie even if he could fly. He wasn't even sure if he could talk any more.

"You'd better grow some wings if you want to be my friend," she said as she took off into the sky squawking on and on and on.

"There you have it, is right!" Charlie said. "I can't fly!" he cried. "And I can't run and I can't hop. I don't have wings to fly with. I don't have legs to run with. I don't have feet to hop with. And I'll never have a friend to play with." He was sobbing big tears now.

How could things change so quickly? He had been so happy that morning and now he felt that life just wasn't worth living anymore.

The rabbits came hopping by again. They were playing happily so they didn't see him. He didn't want to see anyone ever again. He didn't want to see the deer or the birds or any other animals. He had had enough. He didn't even want to be in the sun anymore. He must get away. Away for good. He must find someplace dark where no one would go, where no one would find him. Then he could be alone. He didn't care if he ever saw anyone again.

Charlie crawled away and cried. He didn't
know where he was going and he didn't care.
He was almost all out of tears and too tired to
crawl any farther when he saw a cave.

"That's where I'll go," he said. "The cave is dark
and no one will find me there. Not even the sun."

Charlie crawled into
the cave as far away
from the sunlight as
he could get.

When he got to the far
cave wall he climbed
his way up as high
as he could.

"I'm as far away from the world as I can
possibly be," he sobbed, "and that's where I want
to be." It was cold and fairly dark, but he didn't
care. This was the end of the line.

Charlie curled himself into a ball to go to sleep when he heard a commotion. It was people. He had seen people come into the garden many times. He used to watch them curiously, just like he watched the other animals. But now he wanted to be left alone. He hoped they wouldn't see him.

They didn't. They were busy about something else. They were carrying something.

Charlie had always been curious so he couldn't resist peeking to see what was happening.

A couple of men were entering the cave carrying a long, white sack. Some women came in with them, moaning and crying. They very gently lay the sack on a stone slab. The women came over and opened the sheet. There was a man inside. He was dead.

The women took some long linen
strips of cloth and began to wind them
slowly around the dead body. It didn't
take them long but Charlie felt very
sad watching them. When they were
finished they reluctantly started to
leave the cave.

Charlie looked at the wrapped body laying there and he felt even sadder. It had been a very strange day. It was happy at the start but it was ending with great sorrow. Charlie wondered if the man had been as sad as he was because he couldn't find a friend.

But no. The man had a friend. He had friends who came and wrapped him. He looked at the white, linen covered body and thought how lucky he must have been to have friends. "Maybe, they'll be my friends," he thought, "now that they lost their friend. I'll be a good friend to them. I'll make them happy."

Charlie was feeling excited
again. He would give friendship
one last try. He took a deep breath
so as to call out as loud as he could.
But, before he did, a huge stone
was rolled across the entrance
of the cave.

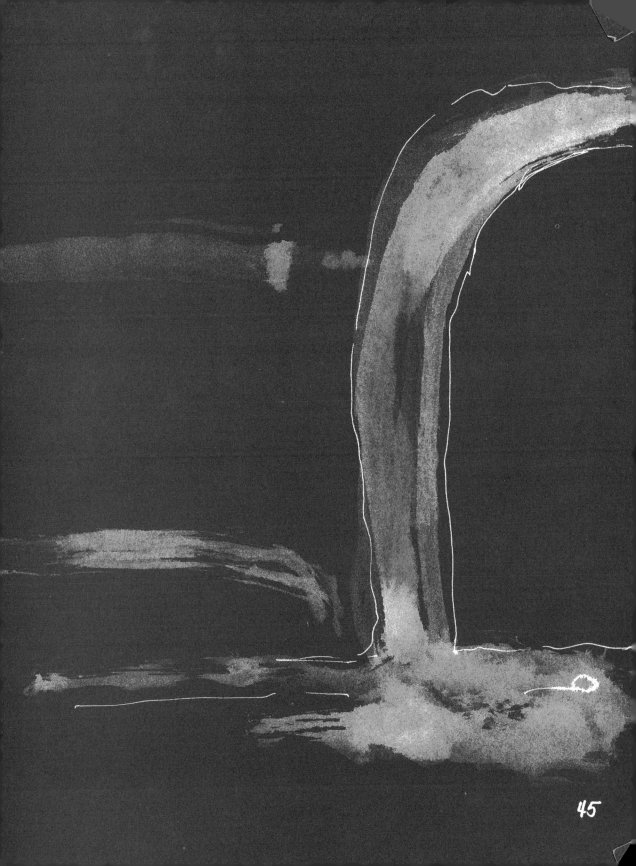

45

It was dark. Darker than any night he could ever remember. There was no light from the sun, or the moon, or the stars. It was dark and it was getting cold. It was all over for Charlie.

How he wished he had made a friend.
He would have been happy with just one friend.
Even when he crawled into the cave, he really
still hoped he would find one. Now, with the
cave sealed there was no hope of that anymore.

The cave was getting colder. Charlie remembered how the women had wrapped the man in linen strips. He knew how to weave linen himself. He had done it a few times just for the fun of it. If he didn't do something soon he would be too cold to do anything. He began to spin linen and slowly wrap it around himself just as he had seen the women do.

"Even this I have to do alone," he said.
"If only I had found a friend."

When he was finished, Charlie was too cold and too tired and too sad to do anything else but sleep. If he could see in that cold, dark cave, Charlie would have seen that he was laying on the ledge above the dead man, wrapped in an identical shroud.

Charlie had no idea how long he lay there. It may have been days or years. Suddenly there was a brilliant light. It shone clear through Charlie's linen covering. It shone so brightly that Charlie wanted to close his eyes. Then he realized that they weren't open yet. He felt warm, too.

Wonderfully warm. Warm inside and out. But, best of all, he felt good. Really good. Better than he had ever felt before. This was all so strange. Charlie opened his eyes and looked out through his linen covering.

The man who had been laying beneath him was now standing in front of him. The linen strips the women had wrapped him in were laying at his feet.

He was looking at Charlie, and Charlie could
see him through his linen covering.

Charlie wanted to tell the man about his troubles and about how desperately he had looked for a friend. Somehow, just looking into his eyes told him that the man already knew. He knew everything. For the first time in his life Charlie felt certain that, at last, he had found a friend.

Then, the man spoke to him. He didn't speak with his lips the way you would expect, but Charlie heard him just the same. He said, "You had no friend so you wrapped yourself in a shroud. I will be your friend and free you."

The man reached up and touched the
linen web. It burst open. Then he
turned and walked to the entrance
of the cave. The stone rolled away
by itself. The warm morning sun
filled the cave. It poured over
Charlie and made him feel good
once again.

"I mustn't lose my new friend,"
Charlie thought. "I'd better go after
him before it's too late. I must hurry!"

But how does a caterpillar hurry?
Charlie struggled frantically to get free
of his shroud. When he started to
crawl he noticed it.

He had feet! He actually had feet. Real
feet. Not big feet like a rabbit... but,
feet none the less. And they were on legs!
Charlie had legs! Long, beautiful legs with
joints in them. He stood up. He was a little
wobbly. After all, he never had legs or feet
before. He flexed his legs and stamped
his feet. This was wonderful!

Wait till the rabbits see him. His legs may not be as strong as a deer's but they were just right for him. No more crawling around on his belly. No more taking forever to get from here to there. Now he could just walk. Just one foot after another like everybody else.

But, climbing down was going to take some getting used to. He had crawled his way up the ledge. How was he going to get down with feet and legs?

"One foot after another, I suppose," he said as he walked head first over the edge. He didn't cling to the stone as he expected. Instead he fell. He was moving head first toward a catastrophe.

Charlie could remember thinking at that moment, "I need help. Friend! Where are you?"

Just before he struck the ground, Charlie suddenly...

...began to fly.

He was flying! He was actually flying like a bird.

He had wings. Wonderful wings. Wings as strong as the wind and as colorful as the rainbow.

Charlie thought his heart was going to burst with joy. He must go and find his friend. He must tell him and thank him. He must tell everyone.

He must show the rabbits his feet and the deer his legs. He must find the magpie and shut her up long enough to tell his wonderful story. He must tell the whole world his good news.

Charlie flew off to find his friend. On the way he would tell everyone his wonderful tale. And whenever someone would ask him, where his friend was, Charlie would

say . . .

"He told me before he left the cave, that he would be with me always, until the end of time."